A Pony's Tale

by Jodi Huelin
illustrated by Ken Edwards

SIMON AND SCHUSTER

First published in Great Britain in 2004 by Simon & Schuster UK Ltd. Africa House, 64-78 Kingsway, London WC2B 6AH

Previously published in 2003 by HarperFestival, Harper Collins, USA. Text and illustrations © 2003 Hasbro, Inc. All rights reserved.

A CIP catalogue record for this book is available from the British library

ISBN 0743489772

1 2 5 7 9 10 8 6 4 2

www.SimonSays.co.uk
www.mylittlepony.com

The ponies gathered at the Castle.
Excitement was in the air.
It was the day to begin this year's Pony Play!

"I hope I get a part in the play," said Minty.
"Me, too," said Pinkie Pie.
All of the waiting was making her nervous.

"I want to play someone important," said Rainbow Dash.
Wysteria didn't want to be *in* the show.
She preferred a role behind the scenes.

Soon, all of the ponies' wishes came true.
"Look!" squealed Minty. "I get to play a clown!"
"I will play the princess!" exclaimed Rainbow Dash.

"I get to be a ballerina!" said Pinkie Pie.
Wysteria was excited.
She would design all of the sets for the play.
Painting was her specialty.

Rainbow Dash..... Princess
Pinkie Pie .... Ballerin

The Crew
Cotton Candy ..... Director
Wysteria ...... Set Desi
Kimono ......

Cotton Candy was chosen to be the director.
She was a natural storyteller.

The ponies got down to work.
They practised every day, rain or shine.

Cotton Candy wanted the play to be perfect.
She took her job as director very seriously.
She followed the script exactly.

"Let's play a game in one of the scenes,"
suggested Sunny Daze.
"We can't," Cotton Candy said.
"That's not in the script."

"I think the princess should sit on a throne,"
said Rainbow Dash.
"No, that won't work," said Cotton Candy.
"The script says the princess should stand."

"I could tell a joke!" Minty suggested.
"Clowns are perfect joke-tellers."
Cotton Candy wasn't so sure.

Cotton Candy liked the sets, but she asked Wysteria,
"Can they be more like the ones described in the script?"

"I think Wysteria's set designs are beautiful!" said Minty.
"Me, too," added Rainbow Dash. "I wouldn't change a thing."

"If we pay perfect attention to the script,
our play will also be perfect!" Cotton Candy said.
She didn't realise that the other ponies' suggestions
might make the play even better.

With just a few days to go until the play,
Cotton Candy noticed something.

The ponies were still working hard on the play,
but they didn't seem excited about it anymore.

I should have listened to my friends, Cotton Candy realised.
They all had great ideas. So what if we don't follow the script
perfectly. If we add in everyone's ideas, the play will be better
than perfect – it will be FUN!

So Cotton Candy called a meeting.

"I want to apologise," said Cotton Candy.
I didn't listen to your ideas because I was worried the play
wouldn't be perfect if we changed it," she said.

Cotton Candy promised that from now on,
the play would use *all* of the ponies' ideas.
The ponies were so happy.
"Hooray for Cotton Candy!" they cheered.

When the day of the play arrived, everyone was nervous.
But they needn't have worried.
Wysteria's sets were beautiful.
Princess Rainbow Dash sat on a sparkly throne.

Everyone laughed at Minty's joke,
and played along with the game that Sunny Daze invented.

"A Pony Tale" was a wonderful success.
"Thanks to wonderful friends!" said Cotton Candy.